GREG LEWIS

CHASING WONDER

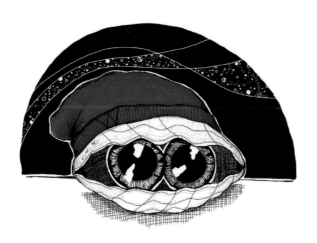

IF WE DARE,
WONDER TAKES US EVERYWHERE.

Printed in the United States of America

First Printing, 2020

ISBN: 978-1-09-835567-8

Illustrations by Thea Goldman
Cover design and layout by Bygrove Studio

Visit www.ChasingWonderBook.com

TABLE OF CONTENTS

Luke –
Wonder is the bridge
to everything.

Cyrus Lewi

For everyone I love.
Know me by my words.

Part One

OUT AND ABOUT

"Wonder is the beginning of wisdom."
Socrates

Chapter 1

Sea for Yourself

Deep and wide as the vastest sea
Inside a place called Curiosity
Things are different yet just the same
Even if known by an unknown name
Curiosity, you'll quickly realize
Strips all things of their disguise

So, close your eyes and open your mind
Who knows what's there that you may find?
This story welcomes all inside
Wonder ensures an amazing ride
And if you take this friendly dare
Truth is what you'll find in there

This is a story about making choices
To deny or follow our inner voices
Why, even an oyster confined in a shell
And crammed in an oyster bed, as well
Can dream a world that's totally new
Beyond its bed and short-sighted view

But oysters prefer same to new
They never change what they do
Sameness, they think, is the source of contentment
And difference the cause of all resentment
Not this. Not that. Not anything new
They're tied in "nots" in all they do

Until one day, when a strange thing happened
To one young oyster, while he was nappin'
This young oyster, small, but just like all the others
Rested in bed beneath a wave of covers
Till he suddenly awoke to grumbling voices
Commenting on his odd apparel choices

"You have a hat atop your head," one grumbled
"It's weird and it's strange," another mumbled
In fact, it was a distinctive knit chapeau
Bright red and stylish, as chapeaus go
But how did a red cap get perched up there?
When and why, from where to wearer?

So, this is the story about the oyster with the red cap
And how small things can cause a very big flap
It's also a tale about good and bad, happy and sad
And wandering about like a lone nomad
It's about making friends and avoiding enemies
And strange creatures and secret identities

But most of all it's about discovery
Why you're you, and you're not me
It's a story about wisdom too
And how we're shaped by what we do
And Wonder is the reason for this rhyme
So, just let yourself wonder all the time

Chapter 2

It's All About Hattitude

There are many famous hats in history
Sherlock Holmes' was framed in mystery
Abe Lincoln wore a stovepipe hat
And Davey Crockett a coonskin cap
A soldier might wear a green beret
So why can't an oyster's red cap be okay?

Well, it turns out that the answer was
The worst of all--just because
But what does that really, actually, truly mean?
Just because... it could be seen?
Just because... it happened to be?
Just because... it's you, not me?

A reason takes thought to prepare it
Blurting "Just because" lacks any merit
Power over others doesn't make wrong things right
Especially if that power is based on fright
But power's what the other oysters claimed
When "Get out now" was what they exclaimed

Why did they say that? It didn't matter
They were mad as the maddest hatter
Irrational thinking held the day
Indeed, all logic had lost its way
Years later, now, we know the reason why
Because that red cap dropped from the sky

On that day strange winds began to blow
And a twisting squall swept very low
Its greedy hands reached way down
To grab all things loose around
Including a smallish cap of bright red
That it snatched from a lost doll's head

And then that fateful random gust
Alive with airborne wanderlust
Carried the tiny cap across the sky
As if that bright red cap could fly
On delicate wings of knotted thread
Destined for a young oyster's head

Until the wind abruptly paused
Which caused
The cap to drop
And plop
Into a rapidly receding tide
From wind to water for another ride

That red cap floated out on a ripple
Like a dangling participle
(A phrase with its noun unknown)
Adrift, misplaced, and all alone
Until it drifted out, into the sea
And sank from its wave-tossed apogee

And just below was the oyster bed
Where that cap, so brightly red
Snagged tightly on our oyster's head
Held forever by knots of tangled thread
Which made the others there gasp with dread
As anxiety, quite unfounded, quickly spread

The other oysters, rest assure
Didn't like this strange couture
And one by one they started to stare
At the startled oyster, uneasily aware
Of a rising tide of harsh resentment
And rumbling waves of discontentment

Matters quickly grew thorny; tensions arose
As every oyster thumbed its nose
(Well, not in fact, just figuratively
As oysters can't, in reality
For they all lack thumbs and noses
And legs and feet and even toeses)

And then an old and crusty oyster pouted
"No bed head better be red," he shouted
"He's not like us; send him away
He's not the same; so, he can't stay"
Then, all the oysters started to chant
"No, he can't. No, he can't!"

The rants got uglier and even louder
"Go away, you're not allowed here!
Difference isn't accepted in this bed!
Expel him now" is what they said
"You have to go; you're not the same
If something happens, you're to blame!"

The little oyster gasped, then gagged on fear
"I'm just like you, like everyone here!
You know that's true.
I know you do"
But it made no difference what he said
The others pushed him from the bed

None took time for fair reflection
None opposed such swift rejection
Intolerance was expressed without a thought
Because alike is good but unalike is not?
Why is being different not okay?
Would you have let the oyster stay?

Or force him into a world he didn't know?
A maze of currents in constant flow
Which is what the others did to him
They shoved him out, to sink or swim
And the little oyster was terrified
And sought a place where he could hide

Meanwhile, far below, where all woes go
A sinister fish swam alone, really slow
Those caught in his path turned and scattered
For avoiding Vidi was all that mattered
They fled and hid very far away
'Cause Vidi came to eat; not play

What Vidi sought was the perfect meal
Perhaps some shrimp he needn't peel
But best of all he savored oysters
Young ones most, because they're moisters
He presumed he'd see some, somewhere soon
His favorite meal—morning, night and noon

Chapter 3

Veni Vidi Vici

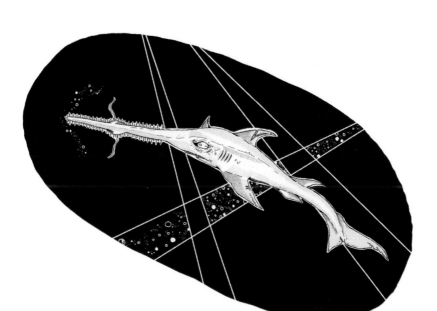

The unknown can be a frightening thing
Open to wild imagining
And whatever is mysterious
Can trigger blinding fear in us
That's when angst invades the mind
And thoughts become all misaligned

Of all the creatures in the seas
There's one defined by mysteries
Why and where and what he'd do
Was feared by all, but no one knew
When suddenly he might appear
From over there... or over here

All sea life knows Vidi's haunting name
Let me tell you from whom and where it came
A mighty Roman emperor of very long ago
A legendary general whom none could ever slow
When his fearsome army swiftly won the war
He coined a phrase known evermore

Veni. Vidi. Vici. Is what Julius Caesar said
Three words in ancient Latin that read
I came. I saw. I conquered. (As all he fought were dead)
So Vidi means "I saw," and now evokes great dread
And every day his legend grew
A fishy tale... but really true

Yes, all sea life had one common wish
To never see Vidi, that fiendish fish
Terrifying in all his aberrations
A ghastly mix of deviations
A sawfish feared throughout the sea
Evil as evil could possibly be

Part shark, part ray, beyond unique
Mismatched pieces in his physique
Extending out beyond his mouth
A sort of sword stretched north and south
Sharp dagger teeth pointed east and west
To slice and dice each dinner quest

Vidi is wickedness to the core
The most sinister fish in ocean lore
His absolute favorite thing to do
Is devour the goodness inside of you
And oysters, he thinks, are the most delicious
The favorite of all his dinner dishes

Vidi believed oyster prey were easy
He'd seize an oyster "before he sees me"
All it took is a single snap
While in their bed, the oysters napped
Just one big bite would end his bellyache
But why not more bites, for badness' sake?

Chapter 4

DISCOVERY

Cast away and rejected; all by himself
The oyster hid alone, along a rocky shelf
He peered at a world he'd not seen before
They banished him, then locked the door
And just because the weight of fate
Had placed a cap atop his pate

Even a nearby sand dollar knew that made no cents
Little things are little things, why make them immense?
But the anxious oyster didn't wonder why, only how
How to make the best of his sad plight somehow
As solutions are what we all must find
When problems occupy our mind

Then one day, things changed on a fluke
So close it touched his bright red toque
A migrating whale swam slowly by
So long and wide, it blocked the sky
And in that moment dark as night
Our oyster finally saw the light

With passing whales as inspiration
The oyster came to a realization
Why not address his desperation
By overcoming his hesitation
And venture out into the sea
Beyond the known and memory

What's the purpose of hiding on a shelf?
"It's time, I think, to move myself
Yes," he thought, "I guess it's up to me
To be... to be... or not to be"
And that's a question we all must ask
Though answering it's no easy task

How do we find the will and strength to go
Into a bigger world we can't fully know?
And how does an oyster ever step out
Without any feet to walk about
Well, no one should ever feel defeated
If they strive to get their tasks completed

So, determined not to be discouraged
The little oyster found the courage
Finally, after an anxiously long delay
He rocked off the shelf and drift'd away
And here and there and everywhere, much to his great surprise
The unknown he feared didn't appear, and delight soon filled his
eyes

He floated along a sandy bottom promenade
Where trumpet fish all loudly played
An opus for an octopus whose eight legs quickly tangled
While a nearby starfish marched in place, to an anthem quite
star-spangled
"Wow," the little oyster thought
"Perhaps my fear is fear for not"

Then he saw a castle beautifully carved from coral
With ramparts jutting up, atop an entry portal
Where swordfish stood as noble sentries
And triggerfish guarded secret entries
That water carved over endless time
A wave-washed fortress so sublime

That reef was like a Broadway show
A cast of characters he'd like to know
A clownfish there for comedy
A shark for melodramady
And the damsel fish, the lovely ingénue
Posed poised, for this was her milieu

Next, with purpose, right on cue
A troupe of porpoise rose up and flew
Guitarfish strummed scales into a tune
A bass joined in on a bass bassoon
And the blowfish chorus began to blow
To welcome Marlin... the one called "Brand-Oh!"

Marlin Brand-Oh! was a superstar, famed on the waterfront
The wild one who, despite his spear, could also be quite blunt
"I couldn't be contenter," he would often boast
"I'm Brand-Oh! you know (not Brand-X), a star from coast to coast!"
The oyster watched intently, really quite amazed
While groups of grouper groupies all behaved so crazed

The oyster never imagined he'd see
So many living in harmony
If this was life beyond the bed
Then he had nothing more to dread
"The others are trapped inside their wrong beliefs
But I am free... to explore the farthest reefs"

And then he paused to wonder, how far is far
Is it close or distant from where you think you are?
How do you know when you are there?
Could far be hidden anywhere?
Is far the same for you and me?
Is far a worthy destiny?

Chapter 5

Esteemed Lobster

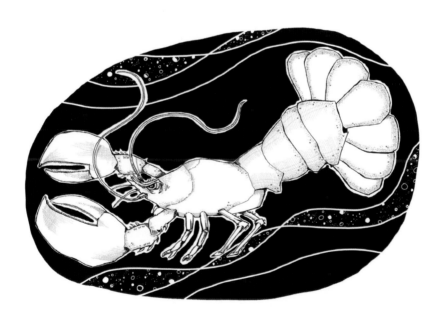

Every night, as evening harkened
And the ocean quickly darkened
The oyster watched the sea life changing
All the creatures rearranging
Those who really liked the day
At night would go and hide away

Nocturnal fish would arrive
And in the darkness come alive
Which leads us to tell a lobster tale
About one humongous lobster tail
And an ego quite superior
Just because of his posterior

"I'm esteemed lobster
Crusher the mobster
The biggest, the toughest
For sure the very roughest
All sea life scatters when I arrive
If it wants to stay alive"

Dressed in a fiery red coat of armor
Dangerous as a three-alarmer
Crusher strut right into view
First one huge claw, and then two
Peduncle and antennae spinning
Mandible wide open, grinning

In the interest of color correctness
And to avoid anatomical imperfectness
Lobsters are green... until they are caught
And then cooked till bright red in a boiling pot
So, why is Crusher missing all of his greenness?
Because he boils over each day in his own meanness

The oyster had never seen this before
Strutting across the ocean floor
A lobster bigger than imagination
In fact, he seemed an aberration
As odd as an oyster wearing a cap

A lobster with a gangster rap
As the lobster drew nearer and nearer
The oyster felt the flames of fear
All that he could see was red
(Just like the hat atop his head)
And as the oyster filled with dread
He knew why the others stayed in bed

"I'm a searchin' for sea urchin"
Said the hungry lobster, lurchin'
Gruff and tough whenever talking
Like a Boston mobster stalking
"Love dem creatures' spiny features
I'll gulp dem all, you can be sures"

The oyster shrieked a frightened sound
Quickly, Crusher jerked around
Inches from the oyster's face
The little oyster froze—yes, froze—in place
What to do, he didn't know
For there was no place else to go

Then, with claws a-clacking,
The lobster started slowly backing
"You're too small for me," Crusher grumbled
Shook his head, annoyed, and mumbled
"Of you I'd have to eat a dozen
Besides, I likes 'em fresh not frozen"

The oyster sighed. "Oh, what relief"
He'd feared he might have come to grief
"Maybe free is not so easy
I know right now I'm feeling queasy"
And for a while he stayed quite still
"I think," he said, "I've had my fill"

"I'm not really made for this?" he told himself
"I feel far safer on the shelf
And what if I return to the oyster bed?
Could they forgive what's on my head?
It's just a cap; why do they care?
It's not a cap I chose to wear"

And then he gazed into the distance
Beyond time and place and his resistance
Might the oyster get stuck inside low tide
Too afraid to explore the other side
Past that edge where what's known ends
Where courage and confidence are your best friends?

"Back... or forward. Where should I go?
What's out there? Do I want to know?"
But you know what's out there—the sawfish Vidi
Awaiting an oyster, young and meaty
An oyster with a bright red cap
Who sometime soon must take a nap

By then, Crusher had disappeared into the dark
On the oyster he'd made a lasting watermark
But the oyster had impressed Crusher, too
And Crusher wondered what he might do
Could he make a lonely little oyster his only friend
In this tale's beginning, no... but what about the end?

Chapter 6

ROCK & ROIL

With the lobster tale all but behind him
And after days of feeling grim
The oyster slowly overcame his fear
(Not knowing Vidi was lurking near)
He decided doing nothing was its own dead end
And that's quite important to comprehend

So, he ventured out, and things went well... at first
He saw crabs and conchs and a carp that cursed
Turtles and rays, sharks big and small
Starfish and startled fish, seaweed green and tall
All was good, as he drifted along
He really felt like he belonged

Then, the ocean currents fiercely quickened
So rough, the oyster got sea-sickened
Tumbling and stumbling, out of control
Inside waves in a roiling roll
And then he ricocheted into some rocks
Back and forth, all very hard knocks

Smack and thwack, a wicked whack
So terribly scared his shell might crack
The oyster struggled against his plight
Shell shocked and shaken with trembling fright
When a gigantic squid jetted into sight
Then grabbed the oyster and squeezed him tight

Circumstances seemed so very bleak
Pressed against the squid's hard beak
Right below his bulging eyes
Black in white and so outsized
"Oh, this squid means my demise
He's huge, I'm small, just right bitesize"

But then the squid pulled the oyster out
Freeing him from rocks and doubt
"Oh, thank you, thank you," the oyster gasped
His voice so weak his words collapsed
"All my pleasure," the big squid replied
"For left alone you would have died"

Once again, in panicked confusion
The oyster had reached the wrong conclusion
As sometimes we read things wrong under duress
And anticipate outcomes that aren't the best
The fact was he wouldn't be that giant squid's lunch
And disappear in one huge, hungry crunch

Meanwhile, the squid was contemplating
What he should ask for liberating
The little oyster from his wave-tossed plight
Should the price of payback be heavy or light?
Regardless, the oyster was about to learn
He wasn't free yet from all concern

"There's a deal," said the squid, "I think we should make
And seal it with an eight-hand shake
You owe me now, for saving you
So, whatever I ask is what you'll do
And when it's time I'll let you know
Remember me! I'm Squid Pro Quo"

For the oyster this was something new
What might he be asked someday to do?
Goodness, he realized, isn't always free
From strings attached that you can't see
And there was something more he didn't know
Vidi, too, had a deal with Squid Pro Quo

Chapter 7

The Sawfish and The Squid

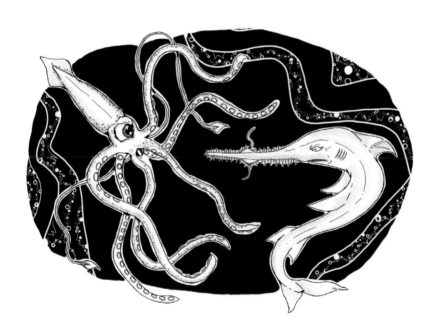

The deeper you go in the deep-deep sea
The darker it gets; the sun ceases to be
In such darkness creatures should beware
The absence of light swallows everything there
How do you know good from bad or far from near?
Without any light, does truth just disappear?

Squid Pro Quo didn't have the slightest care
If it was light or dark way down there
If truth disappeared, it didn't matter to him
He ruled the deep and ruled by whim
Until, one day, while casually cruising about
He felt the swing and a miss of a sawfish snout

It was Vidi, alright; the largest sawfish, by boast
Some 20-feet in length, from coast to coast
And his saw was the longest you've ever seen
Fifty teeth on each side; he was snarling and mean
Each one a dagger designed to cut and shred
In front of his mouth, on the underside of his head

In that mouth, top and bottom, two phalanxes of teeth
Three hundred or more, aligned above and beneath
Like soldiers always ready for war
Each tooth was a gladiator
In the faintest light you could tell it was Vidi
By his horrible smell and his dorsal graffiti

Gouged out of that fin was a slice shaped like a V
V for Vicious, of course... and his name, Vidi
There's a legend about how that V was ripped out
On a night when a Great White was swimming about
Vidi and that shark met each other head on
And at their battle's end, the Great White was gone

The squid knew this story, so why should he fight
He might win against Vidi, yet the chances were slight
His other option—negotiate
But would evil Vidi participate?
So, he proposed a deal he hoped Vidi might take
Exaggerating his confidence to bolster the case he'd make

Thus, the squid stood his water, and flashed a confident grin
"If you want to do battle, I'm ready to win
I've got eight mighty arms that can punch high and low
I can smack you down hard with every blow
I'm strong and I'm tough and I've studied karate
My punches will break every bone in your body"

Vidi replied with a wicked smirk and nasty grin
His whole being tensed like the sinew of sin
"My saw blade sizzles with spikes hot as lasers
I'll filet you in seconds, my snout's studded with razors
You have eight arms now, but you won't when I'm through
You'll have none left, or at best one or two"

According to legend the standoff went on... and on
Incendiary insults... fiery threats till past dawn
Those deep chilly waters warmed up by bravado
A cold war gone hot, enflamed by one desperado
And a squid who wished to avoid any fight
By pretending to be dangerous as dynamite

Explosive affronts were thrown back and forth
Bombast and lambast whatever that was worth
I'm this—You're that—I won't—You will
Insults were traded, evermore shrill... until
"Let's make a deal," the squid finally proposed
The two of them positioned nose to nose

"You go your way, and I'll go mine
And I promise, a favor at some future time"
Now that's what's known as giving this to get that
It's what you would do as a diplomat
In Latin the term is Quid Pro Quo
A fair exchange that's apropos

And that's what they did
The sawfish and squid
Though Vidi would always boast that he'd won
Insisting the squid really wanted to run
But the giant squid got exactly what he wanted
Notoriety in the sea, for appearing undaunted

Now, considering the size of all the oceans
And how time and distance soothe emotions
Vidi and squid might never meet again
To battle and brawl and see who'd win
But the seas are filled with great surprises
What seems certain today, tomorrow denies us

Chapter 8

WONDERFUL

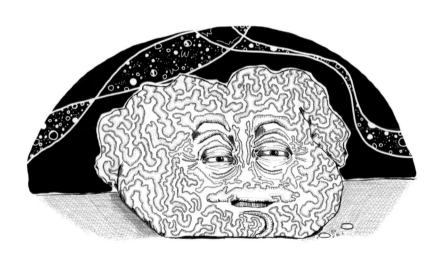

One day in disbelief
The oyster saw a giant reef
In fact, the largest in all the world
That stretched for miles, straight and curled
The Great Barrier Reef comprised all types of coral
And happy fish that seldom quarrel

Even giant sea anemones
Thrived there without real enemies
So, curious to see and know lots more
The oyster decided he must explore
First, a herd of elephant coral
With swimming trunks in patterns floral

Then the highest, the pillar coral, holding up the sky
The lowest was the table coral, lying flat nearby
A bit further ahead a fan coral waved hello
And the staghorn coral's antlers stood up down below
While a brain coral smartly quoted,
From different books he often noted

The works of Shakespeare (a Bill fish) are those he loved best
But it was Hamlet he recited more than all the rest
"'We know what we are, but know not what we may be,'"
(As if he were Ophelia, overcome by tragedy)
"The past has passed; we are our history
Our future is hope concealed in mystery"

Mollusks, in general, are quite benighted
The oyster had never heard The Bard recited
"That brain coral sure is smart," the oyster thought
"Equipped with knowledge that I am not"
"Yes," the brain coral said. "Ja... da... oui... si
You'd learn it all if you learned from me"

"About calculus and calcu-more
Moby Dick and ocean lore
Ravens tapping at my chamber door"
(Poe's; not the ones from Baltimore)
"You'd read the works of Sophocles
And study distant galaxies"

"Yes, I'm a coral so erudite
My theories are all watertight
My thoughts can dance to algorithms
Like inconvenient truths—all Al Gore-isms
Bake (apple) pi or recite it
Advise Adam not to bite it"

"I'm so smart," the brain coral said
"All of knowledge is in my head
Through logic I know how to marry
What comes first, then secondary
Like, if you worry, it makes you wary
And that's why I'm called Coral Larry"

"I need no name," the oyster said
"And if I do, just call me Red
What's the purpose of a name?
Red or Blue, I'm just the same.
And, really, no one cares about me
A red-capped oyster lost at sea"

"Lost?" Coral Larry objected. "How could you be?
You left the bed; which set you free
Someday read Paradise Lost
About free will and what that cost
Of course, it's up to you what you do, now
And why and when and where and how"

"But have a purpose. Say yes to know!
The unknown is something you should see, so go!"
And then, the brain coral added for emphasis
"If you don't go, think of what you'll miss
Live your life; feel alive
Do it all; don't just survive"

The oyster said, sort of matter-of-fact
"I guess it's courage that I've lacked
I start then stop, instead of trying
Why go? Why not? I can't stop why-ing
I wonder... I wonder if good or bad is lurking there
I can't be certain, anywhere"

"Wonder! Yes, yes, that's it!" Coral Larry exclaimed.
"The perfect name for you!" And then explained
"Wonder. WONDER! It's what we all should do
Question. Admire. Let curiosity come through
And if you wonder, then it's wonder you'll find
Awe and beauty of a staggering kind"

The little oyster wasn't sure if that was true
Sometimes it's so easy to misconstrue
"Well, if that's right, what now?" Wonder asked
And Coral Larry replied, "Move passed the past
Wander, Wonder. Open your mind
Seek all the wisdom you can find"

"And what is wisdom?" Wonder wondered
"In its pursuit... what if I blundered?
Where to go and where to look
Where to find the true guidebook
What if wisdom is elusive
And seeking it is inconclusive?"

He paused to think, "Must I do it?
Go forth and eagerly pursue it
Is wisdom short or is it tall?
Does it hide behind a wall?
Is wisdom there for one and all?
And will it answer if I call"

Coral Larry saw Wonder's overwhelming concern
"Wisdom," he advised, "is a gift you steadily earn
School is the place where you get knowledge
But wisdom's a journey far beyond college
You'll understand, Wonder, just give it time
There's lots more for you to do inside this rhyme"

Chapter 9

Au Pair of Fish

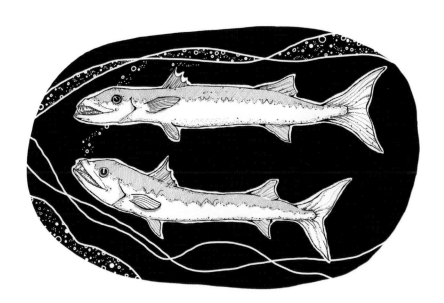

Coral Larry stared at Wonder, unrelenting
Until the oyster stopped dissenting
Then Larry said, with great conviction
"If you don't go, that's dereliction"
"What do you mean by that?" Wonder replied
"Is the purpose of life to take the ride?"

"Don't," Coral Larry continued, "hide from the world – or yourself!
Don't return to that darkened shelf!
Your heart will show you the way, that's right
For the Presence of Wonder" (Thanks, E. B. White!)
The oyster didn't comprehend all that yet
But in time he would – and never forget!

Then, later on, on another day
Immediate danger hid not far away
Tucked beyond a darkened door
Just above the ocean floor
Long and spotted, with tiny eyes
And mouth wide open set to surprise

Concealed inside that secret hole
A Moray eel quietly twists and rolls
His tapered head gliding in and out
Displaying scythe-like teeth in a jaw quite stout
Ideal to crush a shell and shred a cap
And do it all with a single snap!

Wonder couldn't possibly know
That up ahead, where he was about to go
That a hungry eel, that nasty Moray
Loved nothing more than oyster cacciatore
(Amore é tenerezza, amore é calore)
A five-star meal for an eel that's predatory!

For that famished eel
Could glimpse his tasty meal
An oyster looking oh so yummy
Who'd fill the space in his empty tummy
A void no oyster could avoid
A tasty meal to be enjoyed!

Quickly, the Moray opened his elongated jaw
As the oyster turned; shocked by what he saw
A gluttonous eel prepared to eat him raw
To bite and crush, and grind and gnaw
Which are what Morays are designed to do
And to themselves they must be true

Suddenly the large eel lurched out
Those teeth protruding from its snout
And that set off a strange commotion
A cloud of sand swirled in the ocean
Everything seemed so surreal
As the eel itself became the meal!

Barracuda, not one but two
Had chomped the eel and begun to chew
As Wonder spun 'round, his red cap fluttered
His racing mind confused and cluttered
With thoughts his lips barely muttered
"W-w-w-woulda… shoulda… barracuda!" is what he finally stuttered

Then for a moment, numb with fright
A mere shell of himself, he just sat tight
"Phew," he gasped at what he'd seen
His breaths few and far between
"Wow!" he exclaimed to the barracuda fish
"I coulda been that eel's dinner dish"

"My name's Wonder, by the way"
His thoughts still in disarray
Which often leads to wrong conclusions
And loss of Truth amid confusions
So, he paused; until his head stopped reeling
"And who are you?" he asked with feeling

"She's Sara and I'm Dipidee
And sometimes we just happen to be—
Here and there to do some good
And we'd do more, if we could
But it's all by chance; we never know
We can't be everywhere you might go!"

"Well, thanks!" Wonder exclaimed, "You rescued me
From a certain and horrible catastrophe!
Oh, how lucky I must be to be
Saved by Sara and Dipidee
I hope you're around if I need you again
But I've no idea where or when!"

And then the two fish swam away
As good fortune is never here to stay
Just as bad luck won't hang 'round forever
Especially if you endeavor
To push yourself in the right direction
And stop when you should for true reflection

If you were Wonder would you go back home?
Or would all your roads lead you to roam?
Would you return to the oyster bed?
Or seek adventure up ahead?
Wonder decided to explore for more
To sea what life had in store

Chapter 10

Size Matters

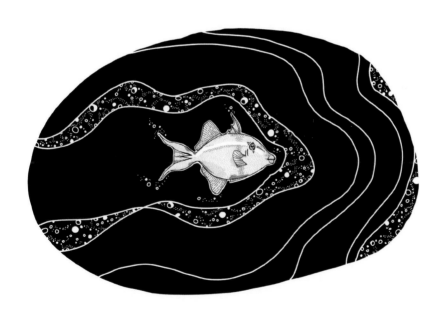

When things first come into view
It can be easy to misconstrue
What they are, and what they're not
If you don't reflect a lot
Which explains Wonder's big surprise
When he met an exquisite fish just half his size

You'd think her bigger than King Kong
When you hear her name so very long
Yes, a name so stupendous
Just to spell it seems horrendous
Twenty-one letters, all in all
Mostly vowels in freefall

Humuhumunukunukuapua'a
It takes some time to say it prop-ah
Two each of H, M, N, and K
Three A's and one lone P, astray
Nine U's are scattered everywhere
But no E's, no I's, no O's are there

(Nor would they ever dare
Leave Old McDonald's Farm and go
Into an ocean they don't know
Eee Aye, Eee Aye, Oh!)
And don't forget the apostrophe
Just before the last "a" you see

Humu is a triggerfish, quite tiny
You'll find it swimming in the briny
With blue top teeth and a pig-like snout
Solitary as it darts about
Known from Molokai to Lanai
Proclaimed State Fish of Hawaii

"It so nice to meet you," Wonder said
"I'm from a faraway oyster bed
I'm..." he paused, "... on my own, now, because
This red cap on my head was
Well... the other oysters did not approve
And it's stuck—a cap you can't remove!"

"I'm sorry," the tiny fish replied
With a voice most dignified
"It's sad they had dislike for you
I've known that; I've felt it, too
Some hate me because my name brings fame
But as reasons go that's mighty lame."

For the longest time they talked and talked
While other sea life stopped and gawked
The tiny fish shared grand ideas
About all of life and what the sea is
Big ideas often come from something small
Wonder is how you consider them all

They even talked of passive violence
Interspersed with thoughtful silence
Of shame and hurt now resurrected
Of being excluded and rejected
 "They rushed to judge me on a false basis
Why do differences make them hate us?"

That's when HumuHumu fairly stated
"Things aren't justly designated
Often, we live in a jealous sea
Divided by what ought not to be
Petty preference. Lack of deference
While life deserves only reverence."

That little fish made Wonder realize
How to view the world with open eyes
What you see isn't always what you get
And to prejudge may bring great regret
For only careful thought will reveal
What's really false and truly real

Know Truth wears no disguise
No Truth means only lies
Greatness doesn't come from size
Or accrue to blamers who demonize
Be open always to surprise
Beauty transcends what meets the eyes

Meanwhile Wonder didn't notice a bigger fish swim by
That gave them both the evil eye
"Hey, lookie there—that little wimpy fish!"
Sneered the bigger fish, as if profound-ish
And then he did two double takes
To be sure his eyes made no mistakes

This fish had giant eyes for eyeing
Both of them perfectly sized for spying
But mostly it was its tail, long and slinky
A tattletale, dark and stinky
It was... it was... Oh, my!
Rattail Ronnie passing by

"It's him, the oyster with the bright red cap
The one I heard Vidi wants to trap!"
And then he took one last excited look
"I'll be infamous in this rhyming book
If I find Vidi and lead him here
To make that oyster disappear!"

With a forceful swoosh he swiped his rattail
Like the sinister thrust of a fierce killer whale
"Vidi will love me for telling him where
Wonder is now, so unaware
I'll be revered as Vidi's trusted friend
All good for me, and... for Wonder the end"

Imagine a world where there is no Wonder
That's just too sad to even ponder
What would become of imagination?
Would all hope succumb to desperation?
Rattail Ronnie didn't wonder things like that
But he did wonder... where Vidi was at

Yet, Humu and Wonder had absolutely no idea
About the spying Rattail Ronnie and his plan to be a
Selfish anti-shellfish snitch fish
Scheming to make himself famed and rich
But greed and vanity have a hefty cost
Some would say your soul gets lost

At that moment Wonder was unaware
Of the proximate danger that lurked out there
He was focused on his little big new friend
The tiny fish with a name without end
Humuhumunukunukuapua'a
Vidi's hors d' oeuvre before a Wonder Whopper

Chapter 11

SOUND ADVICE

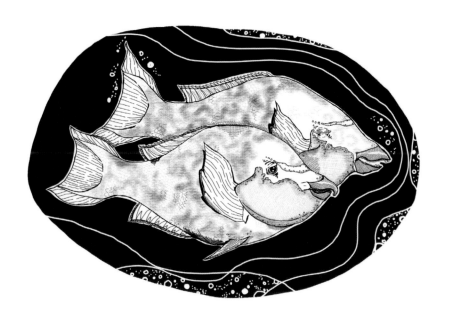

If you've been to Las Vegas
Where neon lights flash contagious
Or Times Square late at night
To watch marquees blink bright
You know why Wonder was bemused
When bright and smart became confused

Though some things flash with brilliant color
Inside they may be dull and duller
Now, parrot fish shine as they go
Each one its own rainbow
But looked at in a different light
That brightness quickly fades from sight

Gliding along the coral reef
Gnawing it with beak-like teeth
Parrot fish bite and then spit out
Bits of sand that float about
Then drift away to distant reaches
To help form all the ocean beaches

And the parrot fish made noises too
A sort of talking as caged parrots do
Though birds have feathers and fish have fins
And one flies about and the other swims
Might they share some common ground
To hear, repeat, not thoughts but sound?

L-O
L-O
R-U-O-K
S-I-M-O-K
M-I-A-B-U-T?
S-U-R-A-B-U-T

O-M-I-M-I?
O-S-U-R-M-I?
S-U-R-X-L-N-T
O-S-I-M-X-L-N-T
U-N-I-O-U-N-I
S-S-U-U-N-I-I

Wonder was totally fascinated
To hear fish staccato, hyphenated
"Are these really words?" he mused
"Or just noise, and I'm confused?"
(Do you know what the two fish uttered?
Was it words or squeaks they stuttered?)

Wonder thought, if the fish swam near
Perhaps he'd hear them much more clear
And soon the pair of parrot fish returned
Saying silly sounds he'd never learned
Spouting syllables small as sand
Hardly oratory, just totally bland

F-U-R-X-L-N-T-I-M-X-L-N-T-S-U
G I-M-A-O-K-A-O-K-R-U
I-M-I-M-4-2-N-8
R-U-F-R-I-M-4-2-N-8-2
S-I-M-2-B-N-V-D
N-V-R-U-2-B-N-V-D

"Hey, there. Hi! I'm Wonder, so...
Who are you? I'd like to know"
But the parrot fish swam on by
Didn't look, didn't say hi
And that made Wonder sort of pout
Though an oyster's shell can't pucker out

Blasé, one parrot fish glanced back briefly
Then drifted on and on and on ennui
Wonder watched in amazement
What had that empty gaze meant?
Perhaps, he thought, they hadn't heard
So Wonder, loudly, spoke each word

"I'm seeking wisdom," he intoned
O-O-O, the two fish groaned
N-F-R-N-F-R -Y-Y-Y
Then dismissed him with a sigh
Initially Wonder felt chagrin
A sense of hurt pride stung within

"Ignore them," a passing turtle commented
"They're not too smart," he lamented
"That's Yada Yada and Blah Blah Blah
Indifference is their greatest flaw
And of course, their vanity
Accompanied by inanity"

"My name is Twain, by the way
And I don't whitewash what I say
I promise to speak truth that's True
Yes, yes, that's what I always do
I say what's right and say it plain
Untruths reveal a character stain"

"That pair of parrot fish
Are the opposite of cleverish
They just repeat whatever they hear
Lots of gossip, not a thing sincere
Beautiful, yes, but they are shallow fish
Go deeper, if wisdom's what you wish"

Then the turtle glanced from side to side
Up and down... far and wide
Like Huck Finn, old Twain had real street smarts
Though no fin like Huck's swum in these here parts
"Fish can be awfully cruel to one another"
Twain warned, as would a wise big brother

"You look like an oyster whose really nice
That's why I'll share some good advice
I've lived more than half a century
Observing things evidentiary
The world is hardly, if ever, fair to all
But giving up ensures your own downfall"

"Life's journey can have an undertow
It's out there anywhere you go
Sometimes all you see confuses you
Uncertainty about what's best to do
Be careful where you sail your thoughts
Don't anchor in a paradox"

A pair of docks? What does that mean?
Something he was sure he'd never seen
There was so much he didn't know, still
But for all of us there always will
The more we learn, the less we know
That's a paradox that's apropos

And then Twain swam up and away
As the advice that he had shared that day
Sank into Wonder's evolving perspective
Raising thoughts quite introspective
Who and what am I today?
What I think... or what others say?

Certainly Vidi, the sawfish so oyster-obsessed
Didn't think beyond his next oyster quest
He loved all types of oysters, often best in a stew
Savored them plump, raw, and juicy too
Oh, to dine on that oyster and swallow him slow
That's why he'd chase Wonder, wherever he'd go

And what about Yada Yada and Blah Blah Blah?
Do they even think about what they see or saw?
Do some creatures live with an empty mind?
On food for thought they've never dined
Or, perhaps, they just don't care
Living life, unaware

How about you?
What's your point of view?
Want to know?
Yes... or no?
Do you have curiosity?
What would you like to learn and see?

Chapter 12

TUNING IN

Neptune is the planet farthest from the Sun
Neptune in mythology is god of the ocean
Then there's NepTune the rapper, the coolest aqua-man
Who raps saltwater rhyme like no other can
A hip hop with a trident who rules in 4/4 time
His message and his music soundin' so very fine

"Yo, the ocean's big and blue
That you knew. You knew. You knew.
But lots of things you don't I do
Things eons old and stuff brand new
'Cause I'm the dude in this sea, ya see
All things down here admire me"

The ocean sways to NepTune's rhythm
All plants and creatures in tune with him
And as he glides from side to side
He sways the ocean's rising tide
And when his fans wildly wave
Surfers get the waves they crave

"Gotta have good attitude
Don't be rude, never crude
Rectitude, fortitude
Gotta, gotta be accrued
At the bestest magnitude
And that's not a, nada platitude"

NepTune was known to all through lore
Famous in the seas from shore to shore
That wild hair, those wilder eyes
A look that could hypnotize
Waist up, a mighty powerful man
Waist down, a fishtail wide in span

His muscled body drenched in bling
Galleons of gold a-dangling
Plus, flashy jewels from sunken treasure
Dozens of diamonds... dazzling pleasure
And on his fingers a score of flashy rings
Sparkle just like the verse he sings

NepTune's beat was the ocean's
His rap the changing tide's emotions
The song of how the sea behaves
The spirit of all the oceans' waves
He'd even rapped with Moby Dick
Wrapped in ropes from a harpoon stick

NepTune didn't foretell tomorrow
Or hang on to the past with sorrow
He only seized the moment—now!
An instant both old and new, somehow
And as he explained it all in rap
All who could hear him began to clap

But the clap of fish is very muted
Because applause that's wet is sound diluted
So, across the waters, blue and salted
NepTune's rap was moistly exalted
His voice could reach the highest C's
In harmonies of the ocean's mysteries

"Nothing," he advised, "can control the oceans
Though winds may try in swirling motions
Even hurricanes, fierce as they may be
Can't rule the life of any sea
Nature has its mysterious ways
That's how nights turn into days"

And among those myriad mysteries
The one with the darkest of histories
Is Vidi, unyielding, as NepTune knows
With evil intentions wherever he goes
Vidi, that name, a single word
Leaves the ocean quite disturbed

Part Two

DEEP INSIDE

"The more I wonder, the more I love."
Alice Walker, *The Color Purple*

Chapter 13

RHYME OR REASON

Wonder happily felt NepTune's beat
Awakened, now, from his own deep sleep
And when he opened up his eyes
Very much to his surprise
All those he'd met were gathered round
Undulating there to NepTune's sound

But how and why? Wonder wondered
Too spellbound to utter even one word
How could they all be there?
Each of them, from everywhere
Might Wonder be inside some crazy dreams
Where what he sees isn't what it seems?

Then NepTune spun, still rapping
Toward Wonder, fresh from napping
"Let me begin by ending your confusion
Don't rush in life to any conclusion
Sometimes Truth is conspicuous
Sometimes Truth must be revealed to us"

"But everyone you've met, all of them are here
All of them, all of them, here from far and near
From beyond the limits, the walls of space and time
I rapped them up, take note, like words inside a rhyme"
With that, NepTune pushed his arms out straight ahead
Head down, thumbs up, his bejeweled fingers spread

Wonder, glancing in each direction
Indulged in sweet and rich reflection
Over there was Marlin Brand-Oh, looking cool and famous
And nearby Crusher, smirking, forever shameless
Thoughtful Coral Larry, smartly in the know
Had sponged a ride (for a price of course), with passing Squid Pro
Quo

The scene was rich with déjà vu
All Wonder's acquaintances, old and new
Humuhumu had travelled there from far away
And Yada and Blah brought their naivete
Twain would arrive later Wonder heard
Turtles are never an early bird

No one had seen Sara and Dipidee there
But, then, no one had a care
And the barracuda were never expected
When circumstances need not be corrected
And Twain, NepTune confirmed, was en route
The turtle as slow as he was astute

But there was someone else nearby there
On his way to the reunion affair
Uninvited and undetected
Soon to be reconnected
Yes, Vidi was there, close by, as well
And one more, too, with a plan to tell

Rotten Rattail Ronnie was not far away
The one who spied Wonder with Twain that day
This was his chance to be greedy, not make amends
By betraying Wonder and his assorted friends
And leading the sawfish to Wonder's party
Right on time by being intentionally tardy

So, Rattail Ronnie slipped away
From this wondrous event that day
To find Vidi and lead him back
Then to watch Vidi's attack
Ronnie imagined himself so very clever
The mastermind of this devious endeavor—

But Wonder was too preoccupied
Danger his happy thoughts denied
This gathering of friends was such a surprise
All this excitement had opened his eyes
But even if you look, doesn't mean you see
Blindness is its darkest when "I" deceives "me"

Yes, Wonder was quite unaware
That danger was lurking nearby there
Having so much fun at his soirée
He didn't have a care that day
Though that would change with a single crunch
If Vidi arrived in time for brunch

Chapter 14

HURRY UP AND ATE

Sometimes the end is a new beginning
The end of losing means it's time for winning
But we don't always know when the end will be
Sometimes it's necessary to wait and see
But Rattail Ronnie was convinced Wonder's end was near
Once he'd whispered where Wonder was in Vidi's ear

As every snitch does, Rattail Ronnie had lots of connections
And he checked with each to find the directions
To where Vidi was lying low, lurking
Yes, soon, he'd see the sawfish smirking
As soon as he told him where Wonder was
Which is what a Rattail tattletale always does

In a matter of minutes once his search did begin
Ronnie spotted a V slash in a large dorsal fin
"Ah, there's Vidi," he excitedly thought, aloud
"I'm gonna tell him right now and do me proud"
So, Rattail Ronnie recklessly rushed to the site
Where Vidi devoured him in one single bite

Poor Ronnie didn't even know what hit him
The saw, the jaw, the teeth that bit him
Before he could say a sentence, he'd vanished
After all, waiting so long had left Vidi famished
Yes, one crunch and Rattail Ronnie was gone forever
Snitches may know stuff, but they're not too clever

Though Ronnie was departed, he'd not be forgotten
And not just because he tasted so rotten
He gave the sea, you see, a brand-new word
That ever since is often heard
The last thing he said as he was approaching Vidi
Was the start of his self-introduction—"I, Ronnie..."

"I, Ronnie Rattail," he was too eagerly about to say
"Have very good news for you, Mr. Vidi, today
Right now, I can lead you to Wonder…"
But annoying haste was Ronnie's fatal blunder
"I, Ronnie…" was all that escaped from his lips
Before Vidi tasted irony on his apocalypse

Oh, If Ronnie could talk, irony is the tale he'd tell
Impatience, as you saw, did not serve him well
As good news delivered badly is easy to swallow
Which is food for thought (which didn't follow)
The news not fed became the news feed
And that's a mouthful of "I Ronnie," indeed

But any day could bring an unusual surprise
Just as Ronnie never expected his own demise
And Wonder was having far too much fun
To be concerned about anything or anyone
The red cap, he thought, changed his life for the good
But there was more to life than he yet understood

Chapter 15

GUESS WHO'S COMING TO DINNER

The moment was nearing for Vidi's planned predation
As Wonder's reunion continued its celebration
NepTune rapped, and they partied rhapsodically
A rap city in blue, by George, performed melodically
And when anyone paused to glance around
None noticed Vidi, moving toward them, inbound

Also there
Half-aware
Were Yada Yada
(So nada nada)
And Blah Blah Blah
Mindlessly enjoying all the hoop la la

Wonder smiled as Sara and Dipidee appeared
A gathering without them would have been weird
He presumed Twain would arrive there soon
From north or south by mid-afternoon
Twain, he knew, never came from east or west
And there's a famous poem that explains why, best

"It's by Rudyard Kipling," Coral Larry said
"Everything he wrote is stored in my head
'East is east, and west is west, and never the Twain shall meet
Till Earth and Sky stand presently at God's great Judgement seat'
It means everything comes out in the end," Coral Larry explained
"The end of what?" Wonder wondered, a question that remained

"The end of you," Vidi thought, smugly
"My tactics are as perfect as I am ugly!"
Yes, Vidi had arrived, exactly as he had planned
Uninvited and well concealed beneath a hump of sand
His moment of glory was mere seconds away
Then... something happened that ruined his day

That's when Murphy's Law began
(And Murphy could mess up any plan)
As the last to be seen on the scene
Was Twain the turtle, usually serene
But now he appeared a bit disturbed
As if something troubling had occurred

But before Twain would say hello
He sought a place to rest, below
Quickly he found it
A sandy mound it
Was, he thought
A perfect spot

Now, Twain was not a tiny turtle
His shell fit tightly, like a girdle
To keep his bulging body in
In spots that were no longer thin
Unknowingly, he settled his poundage down
Onto Vidi, hidden inside that sandy mound

Twain's weight contorted Vidi's spine
His bones and thoughts all misaligned
Crunched now from head to tail
He almost cried a humpbacked wail
But somehow Vidi barely squealed
Not loud enough to be revealed

Twain didn't hear even a single sound
As he relaxed atop that mound
While Vidi's eyes bulged out from his head
"Oh, this turtle must be made of lead
Perhaps that's why they all move so slow
I gotta do something to make him go"

And that's when Vidi burped a distinctive smell
The stench of Rattail Ronnie, straight from... well
It made everyone's nose wrinkle and eyes roll
More proof that Ronnie was a stinky soul
"What's that terribly odor?" asked Twain
"I'm too tired to move again."

Vidi snarled, "When will this turtle ever go away?
I'm crushed. I'm squashed," he thought with dismay
"I'm so close, yet so far; I'm going bonkers
I came. I saw. But look who conquers
A little oyster in a stupid red cap
Because I'm stuck beneath a turtle's lap"

No one heard Vidi's grumbled lament
The muted sounds of a malcontent
Then Twain said, "For decades I've observed the sea
Which has shaped my life's philosophy
I'm old, experienced, very wise
And I speak the truth, never lies!"

"When turtles slowly glide through life
We observe all things, through calm and strife
It gives us time," Twain said, "to focus
To see through all the hocus-pocus
And I... I sense something strange here
I smell danger, and it's very near"

"I must tell you, there's a rumor floating around
It's serious—not something to water down"
Then, with emphasis on every word
Twain added, "Here's what I've heard..."
And then his voice boomed like thunder
Vidi—evil Vidi—is out to get Wonder"

Crusher immediately clacked his giant claws
"I'm ready," he boasted, "to fight for the cause"
The squid tensed; oh, what should he do?
Was his quid pro quo with Vidi coming due?
Wonder wondered what all of this meant
While NepTune hurried away to get a message sent

Chapter 16

ME, MYSELF, AND EYE

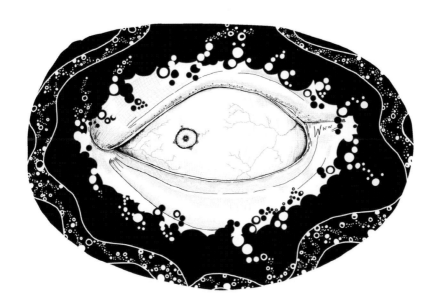

Internal conflict's bad for one's health
So Vidi invariably agreed with himself
Because certainty always made him feel strong
Essential, with Twain on his back for so long
Of course, strong and right aren't always the same
And Vidi always cheated to win the game

The sawfish had no rules or reservations
No guilt, no worry about eating crustaceans
Or eating anything else, for that matter
As nothing tastes worse than a mouthful of ratter
Though swallowing Ronnie made Vidi briefly content
His belly gurgled and emitted an awful scent

At the same time, Wonder was full of pleasure
The opposite of Vidi, by every measure
Wonder embraced the essence of Love and Truth
Vidi embodied the very worst of uncouth
Wonder had friends and ideas... even dreams
Vidi had only anger and hate, it seems

Vidi, as you know, thought only of Vidi
His every choice reconfirmed he was greedy
He didn't care if he ever had friends
He never considered making amends
Vidi had no conscience at all and would never
He lied and cheated in every endeavor

The total losers from all Seven Seas
Clung to Vidi like germs to disease
Nasty creatures with spiteful faces
That dwelled in foul holes where all ocean waste is
The disgraceful, despicable, the disgusting too
Responded to Vidi like fever to flu

But Vidi couldn't get Squid Pro Quo's attention
It seemed like an act of defiant intention
Or maybe, Vidi thought, he doesn't know I'm here
"Under this turtle, even though I'm so near"
Though Vidi could see him, in his (eight) arm-chair
The squid still appeared to be unaware

Vidi needed to alert the squid—Hellōōōō!?
Without letting Twain, still atop him, know
But he couldn't yell or raise his tail, high
So, he just lay there, wildly batting an eye
As only one eye was above the sand
Things just weren't going as Vidi had planned

"Look over here" his eye was silently screaming
"Here!" But the squid was oblivious to Vidi's scheming
"You owe me, and it's time to collect
Don't act now like you don't recollect
Hurry; use those tentacles you're sitting on
Eight arms provide you with plenty of brawn"

"C'mon, get this turtle off me before it's too late
I'm squished under here and I can't take the wait
And don't think for a second you can break our deal
Try that and, you'll see, I'll make you my meal"
But nothing happened, nothing at all
The squid didn't answer Vidi's eye (phone) call

The squid hadn't noticed Vidi's eye, enraged
His mind was elsewhere, disengaged
He'd seen the sawfish only that one time
Way back in Chapter 7 of this rhyme
But their deal—their long-ago quid pro quo
Had changed the squid, in ways you should know

Since then many things had occurred
Good and bad were sometimes blurred
What once were the honored skills of negotiation
He'd honed more and more for manipulation
He purposely contrived to do a favor for you
So you would owe him a favor or two

Recall that fateful day with Wonder
When the currents dragged the oyster under
Trapping him tight between the rocks
After all those back-and-forth hard knocks
And the squid suddenly appeared, to extricate him
It was a gambit, in fact, to manipulate him

Surreptitiously, the squid would set a harmless trap
Unsuspiciously, he'd arrive on the scene in a snap
To rescue the victim unwittingly caught
And then make the deal he'd all along sought
The same trick he'd played on Wonder
A quid pro quo and a two-for-one-r

So many sea creatures now owed the squid favors
In return for all his made-up life savers
That he spent most of his trickster days
Collecting the fruits of his devious ways
But over time even sweet fruit will turn sour
And the time was now ripe, the squid's reckoning hour

Chapter 17

Rising to The Occasion

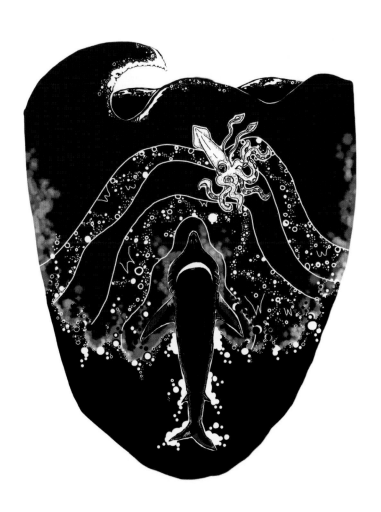

Why does black cause irrational fears?
What happens to logic when light disappears?
As it does in the depths of the sea
Where only a blind fish can actually see
For real vision is more than just viewing things
Real seeing is what understanding brings

NepTune knows what dwells down deep
Where most creatures won't dare to creep
Or even think to cautiously go
Hundreds and hundreds of feet below
Knowing is what makes NepTune cool
Just as unknowing is what makes one a fool

Now, NepTune had an announcement to share
About a visitor he'd invited from way down there
A humongous shark was about to show
Arising slowly from way below
Pushing up like a dynamo
A wave of change that would grow and grow

A wave pushed up by a jaw, so wide
It spanned over three feet, side to side
A giant shark, ascending, ravenous
Her gullet huge, her stomach cavernous
For she had one of the biggest jobs in the sea
To sift through the ocean for dishonesty

She was mammoth, with a wide, grinning mug
A creature so big she could easily chug
Thousands of gallons of ocean each hour
Swallowing what lies there, the source of her power
Gulping the deceit the sea had to hide
An impossible task but she always tried

But while this wave of change bulged upward
And the ocean rumbled as it ruptured
Wonder and those gathered with him
Were seized by the sea's changing whim
Their good sense suddenly capsizing
Judgment lost in the ocean's rising

For when imagination runs from reason
It causes the mind to commit treason
Because stupidity always intensifies
In a brain that fear can paralyze
And exactly that was happening here
Fear staring fear in an infinite mirror

Sea life suddenly spun out of control
The sum of its parts no longer whole
Dizziness struck down everything around
Like the great Dizzy Dean on the pitching mound
A true curveball is what Dizzy threw
A revelation, in fact, and a perfect strike, too

The parrot fish could hardly stammer
A pall of fear eclipsed their glamour
Twain had tried to pull his head and legs inside
Though only tortoises can do that to hide
And Sara and Dipidee had disappeared
Good fortune lost as the great wave neared

Vanished in panic's widening wave
Good judgment was now terror's slave
And whenever fear becomes the master
Then disaster comes very soon after
Logic and fear are always at war
Like waves and rock walls on an ocean shore

Wonder trembled in his shell
Fearing it was his last farewell
So did Humu, Twain and Coral Larry
Cowered by this most scary adversary
Crusher and the Squid reeled with vertigo
Fearing the consequence of what they didn't know

Chapter 18

Big MawMaw

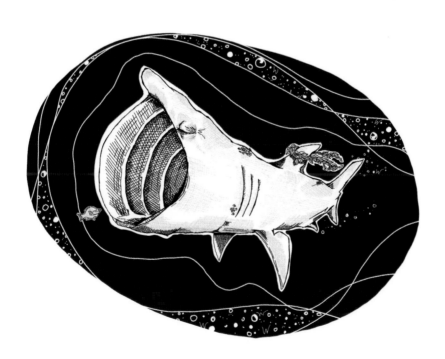

In tides tangled in twisted twirls
Confusion caught in a curveball's curls
Anxiety lingered in ripples of fear
Before current events began to clear
As they all waited, in amazement
To see what arrived from the ocean's basement

Then, NepTune quickly rapped again
"What you'll see," is how he began
"And never ever forget you saw
Goodness. Goodness in the shape of Big MawMaw
For despite her hulk and bulk and wide-open jaw
She's not like those sharks who'll eat you raw"

"Big MawMaw's dental is actually gentle
She's good for you, not detrimental
Be aware but don't be wary
She's the voice of all sincerity
She'll help you get your mind on straight
And take your life from good to great"

That's when NepTune stepped aside
So all could observe, two-why'd-eyed
MawMaw—larger end-to-end and double-wide
Than imagination could have contrived
Her enormous mouth always open wide
To swallow every lie in the sea, inside

Wonder was amazed and perplexed
Wondering now what would come next
While Squid Pro Quo just couldn't wrap
His arms around this giant gap
Of understanding what this was about
His mind was filled with perplexing doubt

Then Crusher boasted, "I gots no fear you's here"
But what he said was insincere
Crusher felt queasy
Bravado's easy
Courage is tough
It was all just a bluff

And Twain was there, alongside
His head inside
Out now
Over and over uttering, "Wow!"
Despite all he knew of ocean lore
He'd never believed in Big MawMaw before!

"Gather 'round," Big MawMaw said
Her voice as deep as the ocean bed
"And I'll tell you about your destiny
Cause I know you like I know me
And I know who does right and who denies
And who makes excuses with lies disguised"

That's when Coral Larry theorized
"She's much smarter than I am, you guys!"
And then, the tiniest of them all
HumuHumu stood really tall
"You sound like that special voice inside my head
You know—my conscience," is what she said

"I am a caring voice inside
Like your own momma's," she replied
"But," Humu said, "my momma looks like me
And we don't at all, as you can see
You're huge; I'm tiny
You can't know me?"

Big MawMaw's voice arose from deep in her soul
Echoing with wisdom seldom told
"Who you are is your spirit, not your shell
It's your ideas and what you do well
It's not how you look with or without a red cap
It's about the path you choose on your own life's map"

Never before
Had Yada Yada and Blah Blah Blah
Been left speechless
By what they heard or saw
And Crusher almost jumped out of his shell
Listening to what Big MawMaw had to tell

Vidi, still trapped under Twain, dismissed what he heard
Being good, for him, had never occurred
What would that ever do?
For evil was all Vidi knew
And so, what if big MawMaw was there
Vidi had no conscience and didn't care

Chapter 19

SHORE ENOUGH

Sometimes it is hard to reveal
Inner thoughts that we conceal
For everyone has secret shelves
To hide things even from ourselves
Things we know but wish to forget
Memories that ache in us with regret

But Big MawMaw possessed a gentle style
That opened doors to our self-guile
Thoughts suppressed in the mind
She helped release by being kind
That's what pulls your backstory out
That reveals what you're really about

"My childhood had lots of fear and hurt"
Twain suddenly, unwittingly blurt
Then, shocked he'd thought aloud—so loud
He felt embarrassed, foolish, even cowed
To have uttered his most inner thoughts
Unfortunate forget me knots

"You're not alone," Big MawMaw consoled
"But you're safe to share your story untold"
Twain paused to glance around at everyone there
Now aware
"Okay... Okay. You all can stay
You can listen to what I say"

Big MawMaw smiled from here to hear
As all the others gathered nearer
Encouraging the turtle Twain to start
To share his story from the heart
As heartless Vidi, still under Twain
Felt his patience start to wane

"I started life buried alive in a seaside mound
One of 100 eggs laid there, sand packed 'round
Each of us in our very own shell
Not too bad a place to briefly dwell
For 60 nights and 60 days
Soaking up the sun's warming rays"

"Until we hatched into the light
Ending our two-month night
And then a desperate race commences
All of us with no defenses
We each struggled to reach the shore
Amid ocean stretching evermore"

"We were such little things
Ungainly on our water wings
Stumbling across the expanse of sand
The killing land
Where hungry shore birds swoop down to eat
Their once-a-year turtle treat"

"Of all the turtles in the nest
So very few pass this test
And ever reach the open sea
Where even then we're still not free
For there more predators await
To put us on their dinner plate"

"Only one of each 100 stays alive
And after that if you thrive
You may survive one hundred years
Each day passing with fewer fears
Mostly alone
On your own"

"For the longest time, I felt survivor's guilt
My conscience made my spirit wilt
And then, one day, I decided
Why live a life that's self-derided
I should be living fully—for me... and more
For those who never got beyond the shore"

"You only get to do this once
So, get smart; don't be a dunce
Live right, live well
Do good, don't dwell
On stuff that brings you down
There is no second time around"

A loud silence followed
Which allowed
Coral Larry to reflect
Before he thought to interject
"That reminds me," the brain coral said
"Of another great book I once read"

And then he quoted
A line he'd noted
From One Hundred Years of Solitude
Words that transcend every platitude
And answer questions for all time
Words in prose that read like rhyme

"The secret of a good old age," he would conclude
"Is simply an honorable pact with solitude
Which means its best to engage
Late in life without hate or rage
Fill your world with gratitude
Embrace a positive attitude"

Chapter 20

JEALOUS SEA

Attitude
Gratitude
Depend on how your world is viewed
And so, more quiet thought ensued
As each took time to ruminate
Cogitate, hesitate, and then participate

No one there
Had been aware
Of Twain's back story before
And more
No longer could they ignore
Their own stories, knocking at memory's door

Crusher's shell starting twitching
Inside his head, his conscience itching
"I got bullied and teased and rejected
Neglected... dejected
Shoved around, disrespected
How could I be unaffected?"

"But until now
Wow!
I never ever t'ought 'bout dat"
And for the longest time Crusher sat
His hot red carapace fading into green
One of the strangest sights they'd ever seen

"I guess dat's why I gots to be a bully
My behavior became so unruly
To get even and be rough
Just to show dem I was tough"
And then Crusher looked way inside
To free the Truth he'd long denied

"But, ya know," he began in self-rebuff
"I've really had enough
I'm tired of dis gruff stuff
The phony huff and puff
I wanna make amends
I wanna have some friends"

That's when Coral Larry confessed
Things that he had long repressed
Hidden inside his giant brain
In a tiny corner of self-disdain
The farthest, furthest most distant place
Light years away in cerebral space

"Nobody likes a know-it-all
Until they need to know it all
Then they'd always come to me
Bowing down on bended knee
Contorted with hypocrisies
A waste—praising me like Socrates"

"Oh, Larry, Larry, my dearest friend
How I've missed you," they'd pretend
"All their lies, so transparent
Though they'd pretend that they weren't
But, still, you know, I always helped them out
That's what the Corollary Principle is about"

"And that," Big MawMaw said
"Assures good Karma is ahead
As everything nice you do
Gets stored in Fate, just for you
Yes, all good deeds done today
Return to you, some time, some way"

"Oh, sure. Oh, yeah. What baloney
That Karma stuff is really phony"
Thought Vidi, still squished under Twain
"I did good… once, and just got pain
When it comes to wrong and right
Badness is what gives me delight"

Soon, Humu started softly talking
"I hated the envy, and the gawking
They made me so self-conscious
And I really didn't want this
Beauty sometimes brings attention
And things I truly hate to mention"

That's when NepTune interjected
"Just as I suspected
You were disrespected
And that must be corrected
Don't just try alone to cope with it
Always reveal what's inappropriate"

The giant squid was now deep in thought
About good and bad in what he'd sought
"I've lived a life of manipulation," he revealed
"Please forgive me for what I've concealed"
The squid was looking deep inside
At truths he had so long denied

"There's nothing wrong with a quid pro quo
If it's a fair deal, it's good to go
But if it's not good, which it might be
You'll burden your conscience with what's ugly
Make only fair deals wherever you go, and know
A wrong deal is a bad deal and it's called a Squid Pro Quo"

Vidi almost lost his lunch, right then and there
(But he hadn't eaten lunch yet, as you're aware
And Rattail Ronnie was so itty bitty)
"What a mouthful of stupidity
What works for me is always fair
As for the other guy, I don't care"

And then Vidi's one eye twisted up at Twain
"This turtle's making me insane
He's crunching me from end to end
I'm not sure if I can ever bend again
But when he gets up off my back
Ah, yes, that's when I'll attack"

Oh, what a horrific surprise was about to occur
But no one was aware; they just were a-whirr
All amazed by what they'd heard
The wisdom of Big MawMaw's every word
And what they found when they looked inside
The truth for themselves they'd long denied

That's when Big MawMaw spoke once more
"I've heard these stories from others before
It's the continuum, you know, of the ocean's lore
Our own realities we mustn't ignore
And don't be afraid to start anew
Sometimes that's what we all must do"

"A fresh start, a new beginning
Every day is made for winning
To move beyond our old losses
No matter what the cost is
Don't burden your mind with the past
Mine the future, at long last!"

Chapter 21

Proph-O-Seas

In time, it's what we all do
Part ways, Me... You... Them too
And move into a different phase
Of life's unpredictable maze
As nothing stays the same forever
No matter how hard you may endeavor

Before Big MawMaw left
She raised her mighty heft
Toward the sun's bright eye
Between a cheek and brow of sky
And looked at her pupils to say goodbye
As the ocean seemed to sigh

On the surface of the sea
Big MawMaw rolled contentedly
Then dove into eternal night
The depths that consume all light
But enlightenment, she left behind
Illuminating every mind

As Wonder and the others gathered near
To watch Big MawMaw disappear
They recalled her thoughts on ying and yang
The metaphoric ends of a boomerang
The tangled emotions of hope and fear
How right and left duel in a mirror

No one there had dry eyes
Though underwater, that's no surprise
NepTune rapped a brief farewell
Predicting you can never tell
When Big MawMaw might decide to reappear
"As your MawMaw," he said, pointing at his head, "is always right
in here."

Then Crusher gave a telltale wave
Finally feeling truly brave
And displayed his first-ever smile
Freed at last from the need for guile
Before he too disappeared
In space and time no longer feared

Humuhumunuku knew
Now, how beauty becomes really true
Only when it's through and through
Every little bit of you
And then she bid them all adieu
As she vanished into the azure blue

That's when the squid looked over, eyes in a quandary
He'd already aired his dirty laundry
Still, his con lead to a conundrum
How to take something and make it undone
Sometimes past things return to haunt us
And righting wrongs then really daunts us

So, what now? What's next?
They were all quite perplexed
When NepTune said, "Always make time to look inside
And brace yourself for an often-humbling ride!
Looking outside in, it can be difficult to see
But not looking at all is a worser way to be"

Wonder wondered, where were Sara and Dipidee?
Missing somewhere, out in ubiquity?
"No, they'll return if Wonder rightly needs
As a friend is one who does good deeds
That's wisdom from Euripides"
Coral Larry recalled with ease

"I'm thinking I'll also head home"
The brain coral said in a thoughtful tone
"Really?" The others asked, "Now?
But how?
Brain corals have no flippers or fins
So how do you think your journey begins?"

Coral Larry replied
"I won't be denied
I've got the power of my mind
And that's an even better kind
When the ocean moves just right
I'll surf my brainwaves through the night"

Then, as if way far away in the sea
NepTune's voice rapped harmoniously
"Be perspicacious
And tenacious
But never, never be mendacious
Always, always be genuinely gracious"

Yada Yada and Blah Blah Blah
Absently stammered, "a... a... a..."
Their thoughts clearly quite muddled
As any advice left them befuddled
But never will everyone all understand
It's just the ocean's grand, mysterious plan

Twain rolled his knowing eyes
At ignorance vanity often belies
"If rumor is north on your compass," he said
"Then dumbness and numbness are what fills your head"
Misinformation is everywhere!
Deception is the liar's lair"

"Just do what's best.
Avoid the rest
That's all you need to know!"
Which all agreed was apropos
And then Twain nodded toward Wonder
"I'm leaving now; my time is done here"

Slowly, the turtle began to elevate
Thus, freeing Vidi, below, from his wait
Still hidden under that pile of sand
Finally, Vidi, could attack as planned
An oyster entrée he'd hastily swallow
An oyster shell clean and hollow

And he'd devour Wonder's red cap too
A dessert only a sawfish wants to chew
Followed by an ocean slurp
A gulp or two and a gigantic burp
Wonder—swallowed after all this time?
Is that the ending of this rhyme?

Part Three

ALLURE

"When I discover who I am, I'll be free."
Ralph Ellison, *Invisible Man*

Chapter 22

UPS AND DOWNS

Every fisherman worth his wait knows
It's the time, the place, and the lure that goes
Into the water and how it dances
That enhances the chances a prize fish advances
And foolishly takes the bait
A choice that will decide his fate

Sound asleep and completely unaware
Wonder didn't have a care
About the approaching, shimmering, shimmying lure
Tied to a line, to a reel, to a rod, secure
Tied to his own destiny, with allure
And the in-Vidi-ous plans of an evil doer

Vidi came alive now, though dead quiet
Plotting his oyster attack, how he'd try it
From front or back, and how he'd pry it
Open to all possibilities, and why it
Would be easy with his malevolent saw
To add sea horse radish and eat Wonder raw

Through the murk and one squinting eye
Vidi saw his dinner, at last close by
Yes, it was Wonder he could see
Wonder, lost in reverie
As no other oyster wore a bright red cap
So Vidi slid forward to close the gap

The fisherman above didn't know
The drama about to unfold below
The scene underneath that augured dread
For the oyster so far from the oyster bed
And you, dear reader, if you don't like surprises
May soon wish to cover or close your eyeses

Wonder's eyes were already squeezed tight
And filled with the dreams of a beautiful night
What I did, what I saw, whom I met
What I learned and what I'll never forget
Far too many I's to itemize
As Vidi advanced, his eyes on the prize

The fishing lure glided nearer too
As Sara and Dipidee came into view
And Vidi inched forward a second time
Silent as an undersea mime
Suddenly! and just as planned
Vidi's saw jerked up from beneath the sand

The long-spiked snout
Slashed about
Slicing the sea
Incessantly
Thrusting every which way at Wonder
Above and below, over and under

So vulnerable within and without
His breakable shell his last redoubt
While upward, Vidi fiercely tried
His saw sea sawing side-to-side
Near and wide
But always denied

Wonder dodged low then high
Just as Vidi's blade streaked by
A narrow miss
And this
Followed by another
And another

Knowing one more swipe could bring the end
Sara and Dipidee turned to descend
She dove and snatched the fishing lure
He pulled the line to ensure
The hook would sink into Vidi's lip
And hold reel tight and never ever slip

Vidi flailed and reeled as the line went taut
And just as taught
The fisherman reeled a lot
To bring in what he'd caught
A sea scene seemingly surreal
A sea saw seen, so really real

Vidi rising, writhing
A surprisingly wry thing
Wonder watched in amazement
Wondering what it all meant
What fate holds in store
What it means in the evermore

The fisherman jerked his rod back
Then down, to wind up all the slack
Reeling and tugging with his might
While Vidi mounted a desperate fight
He struggled to realize his long-held wish
To catch a huge and mighty fish

Evil, tangled in its own depravity
Vidi battled against the gravity
That pulled him up not down
Thrashing, spinning round and round
Desperately
Vile-lently... so violently

Wonder, looking up from below
Watched Vidi, rising slow
Toward the sun-filled skies
Was this Vidi's sure demise
And is this how evil dies?
When the light of Truth hits its eyes

Looking down, from above
The fisherman wondered what kind of
Creature he'd caught
Then staggered back when he saw it
"The ugliest thing ever! Ever!
I never imagined. Never! Never!"

"Scared me!
Really!"
He confessed, out of breath
As if he'd seen the face of death!
"And, so, I slashed the line
Not me; I wasn't dyin'"

Vidi was nearly in seine
As he fiercely struggled in vain
Twisted in that fishing line
Still confined, entwined
And at the same time free
Slowly sinking into the sea

Eternally anchored in his jaw
The lure flashed evil across his saw
Sparkling with malevolence
A lure—allure of lurid evidence
Vidi, the symbol of all things satanic
Sinking down and down, totally manic

Loathing boiled in Vidi's blood
A flood
Of rage
Nothing could assuage
And as it increased
Contempt consumed the beast

And then they caught each other's eye
Wonder low; Vidi high
Screaming words that horrify
"I am evil; I never die
Never! No matter what you try!
No, Oyster, it's your last goodbye!"

Chapter 23

THE ROAR OF THE OCEAN

Terror squeezed Wonder, tight
As fear fostered fear (Roosevelt was right)
"I'm all alone; I'm all I've got.
What to do now? What not?"
Yes, these are questions existential
With both good and bad potential

But when fearful thoughts fill your head
And your brain is packed with dread
It's easy to make big mistakes
And only one is all it takes!
So, always take time, if you can
Make a prudent action plan!

But sometimes time's sum is in short supply
And our second thoughts pass us by
Just as when the line snapped
The fishing line that wrapped
Around Vidi's snout and fins and tale
And loosened more each time he'd flail

Until Vidi was almost free
To exercise his cruel enmity
And Wonder had no place to hide
Except to wait inside
His shell
But what would that repel?

And, so, Wonder decided he would roar
An exclamation now part of ocean lore
That he would open up his shell
And yell
"I'm not just an oyster; I'm much more!
I don't fear you anymore!"

But can an oyster, or anyone, become free
By showing what he or she
Is… really is… inside
Without a shell in which to hide?
"Either I stand for what I am," Wonder said
"Or I'm just like those back in the bed"

Then, just inches away
Vidi began to sway
His saw
And Wonder saw
That the time had arrived—
The test of what he was inside

That he must refuse to cower
That this must be his finest hour
This is what his odyssey meant
This is our story's denouement
Yes, being who you are inside
That's what takes you far and wide

In a single second of introspection
Wonder recognized the right direction
The compass points that show the way
Six ideals for life, every day
What he learned from those he'd met
What he knew he must not forget

Truth is always most essential
Beauty makes you reverential
Goodness leaves you feeling great
Justice for all must never wait
Equality belongs to everyone
Freedom's quest is never done

Those ideals are the presents of Wonder
Ideas he couldn't let Vidi sunder
So, without further hesitation
He overcame his trepidation
"Now! Now!" he yelled
And inside he swelled. And swelled.

That is when Vidi thrust
His saw slashing with evil lust
And Wonder snapped his shell open wide
To reveal a hidden force inside
A force not even Wonder knew he had
A power to resist all things bad

From inside Wonder's open shell
The place, the soul, where ideals dwell
A searing ray of light
Laser bright, shown right
Into Vidi's hideous eyes
Demon eyes, demonized

Vidi shook with fury
How could he
Be stymied like this
Everything gone so amiss?
And he swiped his tail, tangled still in fishing line
At Wonder, one last and desperate time

Which knocked a luminescent pearl
Out, into the ocean's swirl
A pearl Wonder had grown, unknown
A brilliant force that shown
Warm light into a gelid sea
That heightened Vidi's jealousy

The pearl sank ever deeper, less and less bright
And Vidi fell the other way, as wrong divides from right
Vidi, shouting, ranting, still
"I'll get you, Wonder, yes I will!"
But the ocean swallowed Vidi's threat
Words and ears never met

Wonder observed the tableau below
Good and evil descending, slow
The lure... the pearl. Sinking out of sight
Temptation and Truth—wrong and right
Our choices of the different ways
We can live our nights and days

Wonder took a few deep breaths and then reflected
How he was better—despite being rejected
One never ever knows, he thought
What tomorrow will bring... or not
And then he took one more glance
To see the lure and pearl, per chance

Chapter 24

SEA THE LIGHT

Staring down into an infinite sea
Wonder searched for more than memory
Would recall over time
(Now recorded in this rhyme)
"The pearl! Where is the pearl?" he pled
The question echoing inside his head

And then he saw a glimmer of light
At the distant fringes of his sight
Was it, perhaps, the precious pearl he saw?
Or the lure secured into Vidi's jaw?
It's not always easy to recognize
What's good or bad, where Truth lies

Because both, in fact, are always there
You'll find them here and everywhere
So, before you follow any light
Take time; be sure it's right
The more you leave bad behind
The better life will be designed

Then Wonder recalled something Coral Larry said
Wisdom from another book he'd read
"Life is a sum of all your choices"
[La vie est la somme de tous vos choix]
Wisdom shared worldwide in many voices
But in all of them it's true
This quote from Frenchman Albert Camus

And Wonder realized life sails all ways
Through dark nights and bright days
On gentle seas and seas in despair
And now it was his turn to share
Everywhere, the kindness of all his friends
(Which is why this story never really ends)

Wonder felt his red cap vibrating
The ocean current accelerating
And so, he leaned into the flow
Time to go; more to know
To do. To see
To all ways, always be

All wonder possesses its own pearl inside
Trust its power to be your guide
And there will be allure, too
Dangling right in front of you
It's up to you to decide what to do
Know Wonder will always help you through!

Fín

Can you spot the Ws?

Each illustration in Chasing Wonder contains several W's. These W's are visible but hidden. "W" stands for Wonder, of course. Can you find all 137 W's?

The number of W's hidden in each illustration is listed below.

Good luck. Have fun.

Illustration:

In Appreciation

Thank you to everyone who made me a better writer and Chasing Wonder a better book.

I am forever indebted to my brilliant and inspiring high school English teacher Frank Slevin, who awakened my love of words and writing.

Profound gratitude to Willa Perlman, who edited Chasing Wonder. Her keen attention to words, grammar, ideas, and execution raised my game to its highest-ever level.

And applause for Doren Pinnell. You made it happen. You are the metaphor for all good things in my life.

Abundant kudos to Maria Przyborowska for her graphical expertise and judgement, which is reflected on every page of Chasing Wonder. Your skill, your understanding, and your talent greatly enhanced the pleasure of reading this story.

Steve Tucker is a master of all things digital— from writing code to social media marketing. He is the person in my life who can answer every question and fix every problem, for everything that happens in the digital universe. You are a remarkable friend.

About the Author

Greg Lewis is one of very few poets whose writing has been enjoyed by more than 30-million people. During the 1988 Seoul Olympic Games, Lewis, an NBC Sports commentator, wrote "Legs, Legs, Legs," a joyful rhyme about the different shapes and sizes of Olympian legs, and the tasks they perform. The feature earned Lewis an EMMY award for Writing.

Across his 30-year TV career, Lewis received numerous other honors for writing, journalism, and documentary excellence. His essays and commentary also appeared in a variety of publications, including NEWSWEEK and the International Herald Tribune.

Since retiring from network TV, Lewis has written parody, lyrics, commentary, and poetry. His epic poem, Chasing Wonder, is an unconventional marriage of allegory, rhyme, wordplay, values, ideals, history, philosophy, and joy. Critical readers have called Chasing Wonder a "work of art," a "book of miracles," and a "beautifully crafted, imaginative, extremely clever story, filled with powerful insights into life that will stand the test of time."

Lewis graduated from Middlebury College in 1969 and received an Honorable Discharge from the US Marine Corps.

About the Illustrator

Thea Goldman is a young designer and illustrator currently studying production design at Cornell University in Ithaca NY. She grew up on Cape Cod, MA, and spent practically her whole childhood covered in the sand and saltwater of the Atlantic Ocean.

When she's not in school, Thea still lives on the Cape with her parents and her pet rabbit, Jojo, who all provided invaluable support and critique throughout the illustration process for this book (although admittedly Jojo wasn't very forthcoming with her artistic suggestions).

Acclaim for Chasing Wonder

***

Simply spectacular. The discipline to write this, the creativity to conceive of it and the wisdom and joy it will convey are extraordinary. Sincere thanks for sharing this and may it become a "must read" for children 5 to 95.

Denis Bovin
International Investment Banker
New York City, NY

***

Beautifully crafted, imaginative, extremely clever, insightful and filled with powerful insights into life. You have something exceptional here. It reflects your creativity, your playfulness, your breadth of knowledge and your compassion. You are a gifted poet with an extraordinary ability to rhyme.

Cultivating wonder is the key to life. Your insights into life are all important and worth devoting time to reflect upon and to discuss with others. Every chapter has at least one.

Lee Bycel, Ph.D.,
Professor, Author, Humanitarian, Aspen Institute Moderator
Berkeley, CA

***

This is E.B. White and Dr Seuss for adults, plus a bit of Roald Dahl! I especially am impressed with how the red hat that takes on multiple meanings. How did you ever see this coming? Damn, this is good. You've got a winner. It's a book for sure, maybe a movie. Thank you for sharing this! You put an ear to ear grin on my face.

John Chrystal,
International Banker
Des Moines, IA

***

I just finished reading Chasing Wonder, and I want to read it again. It is tremendously good – complex yet simple, double and triple meanings – humor and thoughtfulness. It is a work of art, fun to read and with the obvious but totally important theme throughout. I am impressed. I loved it and will read it again. Just great.

Rick Crandall,
Author of "The Dog Who Took Me Up a Mountain"
Aspen, CO

***

My impression of "Chasing Wonder" is that it is a breathtaking masterpiece. It is ingenious. I was caught up in the characters and the narrative. I felt the suspense build as I progressed through the chapters. I really enjoyed the humorous tone. The play on words is amazing. I think "Chasing Wonder" surpasses Alice in Wonderland in many ways.

Odette Houghton, MD,
Retinal Surgeon,
Phoenix, AZ

***

I love Chasing Wonder — especially Wonder, Coral Larry, and Twain. You bring characters to life and give them personality, like Squid Pro Quo and Sara and Dipidee. Moreover, your subtle inferences and use of language were delightful.

Jay Skyler,
MD & Entrepreneur
Biscayne Bay, FL

***

I LOVE Chasing Wonder. THE SPIRIT OF Lewis Carroll had been resurrected!

Bruce Paton, MD,
Retired Cardiologist
Denver, CO

***

I just finished reading Chasing Wonder, and I absolutely loved it! I believe it perfectly suits any generation.

Dusan Petrovic,
Graduate Student, International Relation
Belgrade, Serbia

***

The writing was inspired. What a monumental accomplishment to have woven this tale together. I'm looking forward to reading it again. You must share it!!

Dave Brautigam
Hinesburg, VT